SHALOM EVERYBODEEE!

GROVER'S ADVENTURES IN ISRAEL

By Tilda Balsley and Ellen Fischer

Illustrated by Tom Leigh

KAR-BEN
PUBLISHING

For Jacob, Boyd, Sloan and Jane – T.B

Dedicated with love to Ezra, Will and Miriam – E.L.F.

For Sarah –T.L.

KAR-BEN PUBLISHING, INC.
A division of Lerner Publishing Group, Inc.
241 First Avenue North
Minneapolis, MN 55401 USA
1-800-4-Karben

Website address: www.karben.com

Library of Congress Cataloging-in-Publication Data

Balsley, Tilda, author.
    Shalom everybodeee! / by Tilda Balsley & Ellen Fischer ; illustrated by Tom Leigh.
      pages cm
    On board pages.
    Summary: "Grover takes a trip to Israel to visit Brosh and Avigail. While he's there, he writes emails to his friends on Sesame Street telling them about the many things he sees and does while on his trip"-- Provided by publisher.
      ISBN 978-0-7613-7558-6 (lb : alk. paper) -- ISBN 978-0-7613-7559-3 (pb : alk. paper) -- ISBN 978-1-4677-9606-4 (eb pdf)
      [1. Israel--Fiction. 2. Monsters--Fiction. 3. Email--Fiction.] I. Fischer, Ellen, 1947- co-author. II. Leigh, Tom, illustrator. III. Title. IV. Title: Shalom everybody!
    PZ7.B21385Sh 2015
    [E]--dc23   2015017052

Manufactured in the United States of America
1 – BP – 12/31/15

Hello everybodeee!

It is I, your furry blue friend Grover, on my way to awesome Israel! I am so excited! I promised to e-mail my friends on Sesame Street from my trusty blue laptop. I thought you would like to hear about my adventures, too!

Shalom everybodeee!

(Shalom is how you say hello. Also good-bye. Also peace. I am so confused!)

BEN GURION AIRPORT

I am e-mailing you from Israel. I landed at Ben Gurion airport Friday morning. I traded my dollars for shekels. Then I hopped on a bus to Jerusalem.

Brosh and Avigail met me at the
station. Everyone was rushing to get ready
for Shabbat. Do you know what Shabbat is? Brosh said it is the
Jewish day of rest. It starts at sundown Friday and ends at sundown
Saturday. The challah bread at Shabbat dinner was very tasty.

Your globe-trotting blue monster, Grover

P.S. Here is a picture of me on my first day in Israel.

Shalom everybodeee!

Did you know that Jerusalem is the capital of Israel? And did you know it is the holy city for Jews, Christians, and Muslims? I did not know that. Brosh and Avigail took me to the Western Wall—the Kotel, in Hebrew. It is all that is left of the great ancient Temple. We wrote prayers and stuck them in the wall. Mine was a wish for Abby's sick grandmother to get better.

Your wandering, wishing monster-at-the-wall, Grover

Here is a picture of me at the Kotel.

Shalom everybodeee!

Today I joined an archaelogical dig. We looked in the dirt for things that belonged to people who lived there a very very *very* long time ago. I found a fuzzy blue hair, but it was from my own head. I found a dirty tennis shoe. "Hey, that's mine," someone said. ALL RIGHTY! I found a piece of an old water jug.

Your dusty blue monster, Grover

P.S. Here is a picture of me with the piece of a water jug I found.

Shalom everybodeee!

What a day I had at the the enormous Machane Yehuda market in Jerusalem!
Do you know how I spent my shekels? I will give you some clues. I bought:

1. Something that will make our floor colorful

2. Something that will excite Cookie Monster

3. Something that Zoe can dress up in

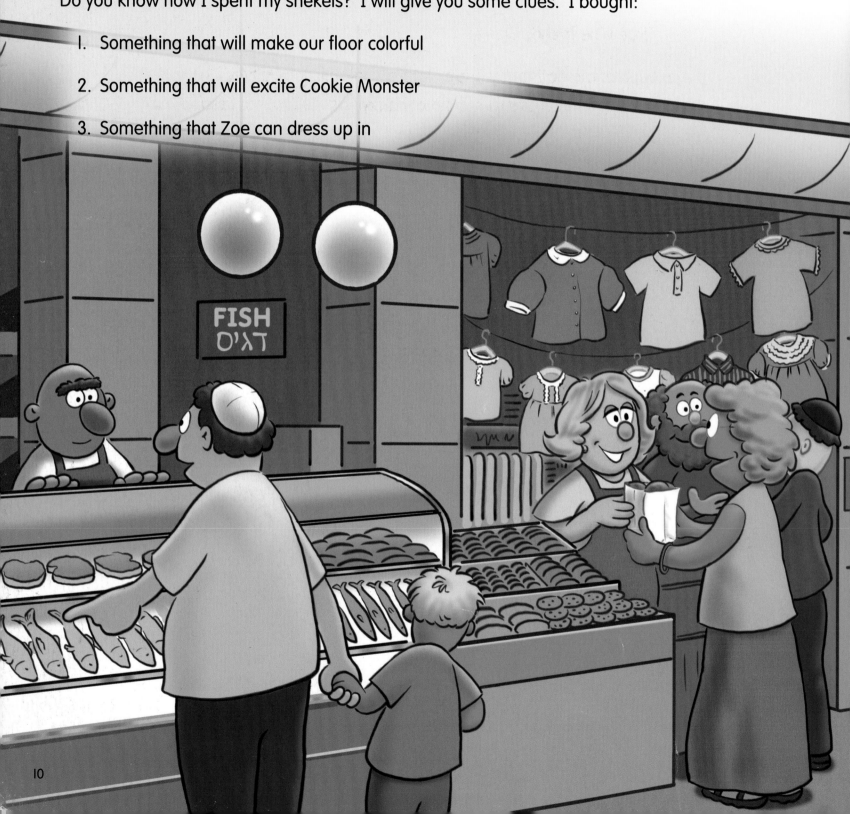

All that shopping made this furry blue monster hungry. Do not worry.
I ate a falafel and a ripe pomegranate.

Your true blue friend, Grover

P.S. Look at me eating my drippy falafel. Falafels look a little like
meatballs, but they are made out of chickpeas. Is that not fascinating?

Shalom everybodeee!

I greet you from Yam Kinneret, the Sea of Galilee. I came to be a volunteer on a kibbutz! Is that not a funny word for a farm community? Of course, some kibbutzim today do more than farm. Some even have factories or make computer parts!

Here is what I did:

1. I milked a cow. I am not so cute and fuzzy covered in milk.

2. I picked cotton. Cotton sticks to furry blue monsters.

3. I washed dishes. I broke only three.

Your sticky cotton-covered monster, Grover

P.S. Here is a picture of me at the kibbutz.

Shalom everybodeee!

Today I hiked up the steep, rocky Snake Path to Masada. That is where some Jews went to find safety from the Roman soldiers a long long time ago. They lived there for six years. It was a long walk up and a long walk down.

Your tired pal, Grover

P.S. You see the speck on top
of Masada? That is Grover,
mountain climber extraordinaire.

Shalom everybodeee!

Yesterday, a mountain. Today, the lowest place on Earth— the Dead Sea. I brought my fishing pole but I could not catch even one tiny fish. Do you know why? Someone finally told me. The Dead Sea has no fish and no plants, just salt, lots of salt. I floated all afternoon. I will mail some Dead Sea mud for Big Bird's sore foot. This special mud will make his foot feel better.

Your salty monster, Grover

P.S. Can you see it is I, Grover,
under all that mud?

Shalom everybodeee!

Today I rode a camel named Fatima across the desert. A long-legged buzzard flapped down right in front of us. I was all shook up, but Fatima never gets shook up.

I visited some Bedouins along the way. They invited me into their tent. We sat on comfy cushions, enjoying delicious tea and pita bread while the sheep and goats watched.

The camel race was fun, even though Fatima did not win. She is slow, but at least she does not spit as much as some of the other camels. Camels can be very rude.

Your furry desert friend, Grover

P.S. My new friends gave me this highly attractive scarf to cover my furry blue head.

Shalom everybodeee!

Greetings from Eilat! Can you imagine Grover swimming with dolphins? I could not imagine it until today. Can you imagine Grover snorkeling? Snorkeling is swimming on top of the water to look at beautiful fish and coral. A mask helps you see and a tube helps you breathe. Is that not totally awesome?

Your soggy furry friend, Grover

P.S. This dolphin is named Dori.

Shalom everybodeee!

Today is my last day in Israel. I am sad to leave and I am happy to be coming home. Yes, it is true. Maybe someday you will have your own groovy adventure in Israel!

Your globe-trotting furry blue monster, Grover

P.S. This is the tree that I planted in Israel in honor of you, my very special friends on Sesame Street.

About the Authors and Illustrator

Tilda Balsley has written many books for Kar-Ben, bringing her stories to life with rhyme, rhythm, and humor. Now that *Sesame Street* characters populate her stories, she says writing has never been more fun. Tilda lives with her husband and their rescue Shih Tzu in Reidsville, North Carolina.

Ellen Fischer, not blue and furry, or as cute and loveable as Grover, was born in St. Louis. Following graduation from Washington University, she taught children with special needs, then ESL (English as a Second Language) at a Jewish Day School. She lives in Greensboro, North Carolina, with her husband. They have three children.

Tom Leigh is a children's book author and longtime illustrator of *Sesame Street* and Muppet books. He lives on Little Deer Isle off the coast of Maine.